W9-BZC-123

THE SOS FILE

THE SOS FILE

Betsy Byars
Betsy Duffey
Laurie Myers

illustrated by
Arthur Howard

Henry Holt and Company
New York

To three favorite teachers—
Miss Harriet,
Mrs. Wiley,
and Mr. Hill

Henry Holt and Company, LLC
Publishers since 1866
175 Fifth Avenue
New York, New York 10010
www.HenryHoltKids.com

Henry Holt® is a registered trademark of Henry Holt and Company, LLC.
Text copyright © 2004 by Betsy Byars, Betsy Duffey, Laurie Myers
Illustrations copyright © 2004 by Arthur Howard
All rights reserved.

Library of Congress Cataloging-in-Publication Data
Byars, Betsy Cromer.
The SOS file / by Betsy Byars, Betsy Duffey, Laurie Myers;
illustrated by Arthur Howard.
p.   cm.
Summary: The students in Mr. Magro's class submit stories for the SOS File about
their biggest emergencies, and then they read them aloud for extra credit.
[1. Storytelling—Fiction. 2. Schools—Fiction.] I. Duffey, Betsy. II. Myers, Laurie.
III. Howard, Arthur, ill. IV. Title.
PZ7.B9836So 2004   [Fic]—dc22   2003018240

ISBN 978-1-62779-097-0
First Edition—2004
Printed in August 2011 in the United States of America
by Worzalla, Stevens Point, Wisconsin

Contents

THE SOS FILE

Have you ever needed to call 911, but you didn't have a phone? Have you ever needed to run, but your legs were like spaghetti? Have you ever needed to yell "help!" but your throat was dry with fear?

For fun and extra credit write your story and put it in this file.

Mr. T. Magro

The Day Arrives

"Good morning, class."

"Good morning, Mr. Magro."

"Well, today's the day. The file is full. Twelve of you decided to participate in the SOS File."

"Mr. Magro, did you read them?"

"I did."

"Which was your favorite?"

"I liked them all."

"Did we get extra credit?"

"Yes."

"All of us?"

"Well . . . all except one."

"Who didn't get extra credit, Mr. Magro?"

"Who?"

"Calm down, class. You will each have a chance to read your story, and I will read the last one.

"Now, sit back and enjoy the first SOS."

The Pink Panther

by Liz Monteon

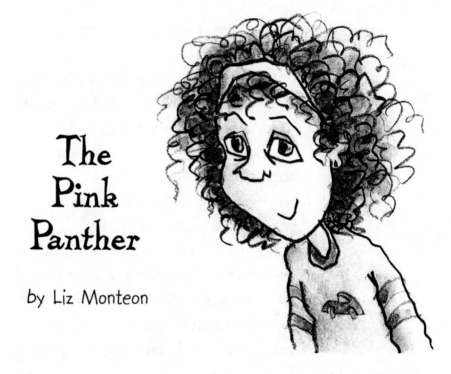

I have the perfect story to contribute to the SOS File. It happened just two weeks ago, so it's fresh on my mind. In fact, my legs are still covered with Band-Aids, and my arm is in a sling.

It all happened on a Thursday, when my best friend, Marcie, and I took our go-cart, the Pink Panther, for a test ride. Marcie and I had made the Pink Panther in my garage. We had attached cool fins to the back and painted her bright pink. We had painted diagonal stripes on the wheels so that when they turned, the stripes blurred into a zigzag pattern. The Pink Panther was snazzy and fast, the perfect combination to win the neighborhood race.

For the test ride we took the Pink Panther to a steep street that dead-ends into a park. Beyond the park is one of the busier streets in town.

Marcie and I stood at the top of the hill, admiring our creation.

"I can't believe how good she looks," I said.

"And the design is perfect," I added.

We had made the Pink Panther a two-man vehicle—or two-woman, I should say. Marcie and I were the two women: me in front to steer, Marcie in back to work the brakes.

"Do you think people will clap when we stop in the park?" Marcie asked.

The park below was bustling with children and mothers and babies.

"Of course," I replied.

Marcie's voice turned serious. "Okay, let's go."

I climbed into the front seat. "When I yell 'ready,' " I said, "you push us off, then jump in. And hit the brakes as soon as we enter the park. I don't want us to go flying into that street."

"No problem," Marcie said. She gave the brakes a final pull.

"Ready," I yelled.

In her serious voice Marcie said, "Countdown

beginning. Five . . . four . . . three . . . two . . . one . . . GO!"

As soon as Marcie yelled "GO!" her legs were in motion. She ran alongside the Pink Panther, pushing hard.

"Jump in," I yelled.

"Not yet. We need more speed."

"Jump in," I yelled.

Marcie was panting hard.

"Not yet. We . . . need . . . more . . ."

Then I heard a scrape, a thud, and a yelp.

I turned in time to see Marcie lying facedown on the pavement.

"Maaaaaaaaaaar-cieeeeeeee," I yelled, speeding down the hill. Objects flew past in a blur.

For a brief moment it felt good, riding in the Pink Panther, the wind in my hair. But the feeling didn't last. I was picking up more speed, and I needed to brake. I reached into the back seat. I could feel the smooth brake lever, but I could not pull it up.

The park was coming up fast. At my rate of speed, I would fly through it and into that busy street.

I thought about steering off the street, but there were cars parked on both sides.

SOS!

Suddenly I had an idea. I pulled my leg up and stuck it outside the Panther. I dragged my foot on the street to slow down. The rubber of my tennis shoes scraped off as I flew along. It was slowing me down, but not enough. I lifted myself higher and pushed my foot harder into the street to get more drag.

The rest happened in a matter of seconds. My shoe flew off and wedged itself between the wheel and the body of the Panther. The wheel came to an abrupt stop, and the Panther swung hard to the left. It flipped over. I fell out, and it flipped two more times, finally coming to rest in the grassy park.

A little kid ran over and stared at me. I lifted my head to ask for help, but before I could, he clapped his hands and said, "Do it again." This wasn't exactly the applause I was looking for.

The results of my ride were: one pulled muscle in my arm, eight stitches where the axle punched a hole in my leg, and lots of scrapes and cuts. Marcie's hands and knees were scraped, too. The Panther was missing one wheel, but otherwise she looked fine.

Anyway, that is my contribution to the SOS File.

By the way, the next week the Pink Panther won the neighborhood race!

Three Strikes, You're Out

by Randy Jefferies

In baseball it's three strikes and you're out. Since I'm not very good at baseball, it could be ten strikes or a hundred strikes, and I'd still be out. As soon as my parents got divorced, my father moved away, and Mom signed me up for baseball. That was three years ago. I've played on the same team for three years.

In all those three years, my father has never seen me play. It's a good thing, too, because there wouldn't be any pride in watching your son drop balls in the outfield and strike out.

My SOS came at the end of last season, when

my father came back to town on a business trip. Normally, I would have been real excited to have him visit. This time, I wasn't. He was coming on Thursday night—baseball night.

Mom told him I had a game, and he got all excited. My father is always enthusiastic. I tried to tell him that I would skip the game, that he was more important, that we could do something special. He wouldn't listen.

He said, "What could be more special than baseball?"

I could think of a million things more special than baseball, but that didn't matter.

I'm sure Dad was thinking I was going to be great. He was imagining me hitting home runs, which I never do; catching fly balls, which I never do; and running fast around the bases, which I also never do. It made me depressed to think about it.

He should have known I was terrible. I am not big and muscular. In fact, I'm shaped kind of like Dad. And he's not coordinated at all. I saw him dancing once. He was in the kitchen cooking, and some oldies music was on the radio. He didn't know I was watching. He danced back and forth between the cabinets. When he saw me, I thought he would quit dancing because he was embarrassed at how terrible he was. He didn't. He just danced harder, as if he didn't know he was terrible.

Maybe I should do that with baseball, play real hard, as if I don't know I am terrible. Swing the bat harder. Run faster.

The night of the game Dad and Mom sat next to each other in the stands. As soon as someone yelled a kid's name, Dad would start in.

"Go, Bobby. You're the one!"

"Look alive out there, Joe."

"Comin' to ya, Matt."

There weren't any opportunities to yell my name, because I didn't play the first six innings.

"They're saving you for the end," Dad shouted. If he believed that, then we were in real trouble.

Our league has a rule that every player has to play at least three innings and bat at least once per game, so at the seventh inning they put me in.

I was sure Dad's expectations had been building throughout the game.

In the seventh and eighth innings I was in the outfield, and no balls were hit to me. That was a relief. Plus, I didn't get up to bat. That was another relief.

Then the ninth inning came. Unfortunately, I was up.

If we'd been behind ten runs, I could have struck out as usual, and it wouldn't have mattered. But that's not the way it happened. This was a close game. We were behind by only one run. There was even a boy on base. There was actually a chance we could win, or at least tie the game.

I stepped up to the plate. I didn't look at my father. I didn't have to. I knew exactly how he looked. Excited! He always looks excited about everything.

I looked at the pitcher. He looked serious, as if he were taking a test and trying hard to think of an answer.

Suddenly I pictured Dad dancing in the kitchen, dancing hard. I thought, I'm going to play like Dad dances. Wild! I'm going to swing hard—harder than I've ever swung in my life.

I held the bat high over my head. The pitcher kicked a little dirt with his foot, then assumed his position. He wound up, paused, then threw the ball.

"Swing," I heard Dad yell from the crowd.

I closed my eyes and swung as hard as I could.

CRACK!

I opened my eyes. The pitcher was looking at the sky.

"Ruuuuuuun!" I heard Dad yell.

I ran. Hard. Fast. Wild. Past first. Past second.

Everyone was screaming.

The third-base coach waved me on.

Past third.

It wasn't until I crossed home that I stopped. I could hardly catch my breath. I looked into the bleachers. Everyone was jumping up and down, screaming. Mom was clapping and waving her arms. Dad was waving his hat in the air.

We won that game six to five. We? I won that game six to five. I. Me. Who never had a hit in my life. I won the game, and I didn't need an SOS after all.

When we got in the car, Dad said, "What could be more special than baseball?"

And at that moment, I could not think of a single thing.

The Chocolate SOS

by Jerry Lee Johnson

My mom would have put this in her What-Have-You-Done-Now? File, but it was SOS to me.

I said, "Mom, I need to borrow forty dollars. Please don't ask me what I need it for."

"What do you need it for?"

I knew she would say that.

"Please, just give me the money. I'll work it off somehow."

"You cannot expect me to hand over forty dollars. What have you done?"

"Please, Mom."

"What have you done now?"

I could see it was hopeless. I said, "The base-ball team always sells stuff to make money. Remember? One year it was wrapping paper."

"Yes, I still have mine."

"Well, this year we were supposed to sell ChunkaNut candy bars. Everybody got forty, and we were supposed to sell them for a dollar each."

I paused, and my mom said, "Go on. What happened? You lost yours?"

I said "I wish" very quickly because I didn't want my mom to start in on all the things I'd lost over the years. Her My-Son-the-Loser File was already overflowing.

"What, then?"

"I ate them."

"You ate forty candy bars?"

"Yes."

"I can't believe you ate forty candy bars."

"I can't believe it either."

"You were supposed to sell those candy bars."

"I know."

"They were to benefit the baseball team."

"I know."

"They were not your candy bars to eat."

"I know. I know."

"Last year what was it you sold?"

"Lightbulbs."

"And you did a very good job. You sold every one."

"Thanks."

"You sold a hundred lightbulbs."

"Well, you and Dad bought some."

"We needed them. The point is that you acted in a very responsible, businesslike way. You went out every afternoon, and you didn't come back until you had sold at least one four-pack. Then you would put your money in the envelope."

"I know."

"I was very proud of you. And the year before that, what was it you sold?"

"That was the wrapping paper."

"And you sold how many?"

"Counting the twenty you bought?"

"Yes."

"Thirty. Thirty rolls of wrapping paper and sixteen boxes of greeting cards."

"And now this! So all the time you were supposed to be selling the candy bars, you were eating them?"

"Yes."

"Where?"

"In my room, mostly. Oh, Alec Hogan ate two. I forgot. I ate only thirty-eight."

"And you think that makes it better? Thirty-eight candy bars is the same as forty."

I knew this wasn't the time to give my mother a lesson in arithmetic. I wisely didn't say anything.

"You're going to have to pay for the candy bars. You *do* know that, don't you?"

"Yes, that's why I came in here, remember? I was trying to borrow forty dollars. I'll do anything, Mom. I'll rake the leaves. I'll cook supper. I'll wash the car. I'll baby-sit Dee-Dee. I'll do anything!"

"I'll have to talk this over with your dad. He's going to be disappointed in you.

"I'm disappointed in myself."

My mom could double file this. It could go in her What-Have-You-Done-Now? File and in the My-Son-the-Loser File.

"One more thing."

I was already at the door. I turned around.

"If you can sell lightbulbs and wrapping paper in a businesslike manner, why can't you sell candy bars?"

"Mom, lightbulbs and wrapping paper aren't made out of chocolate!"

Mom didn't smile. "If that's all, you can go now," she said.

I hesitated. There was one thing more, but from the look on Mom's face I knew now was not the time to mention I needed money to join Weight Watchers. I left.

A Bear Tale

by Augustus T. Bruewhiler III

One day last June, Abraham Lincoln saved my life. You may think that's impossible—he's been dead a long time. Or maybe you're thinking that I mean *another* Abraham Lincoln, not the president. But it's true. *The* Abraham Lincoln saved my life, and this is how it happened.

As we hiked up Little Bear Mountain, Dodger told me a joke:

"There were two men camping in the woods. One morning they looked out of their tent and saw a huge grizzly bear moving toward them. One of the men quickly began to put on his running shoes.

"The other shook his head. 'You can't outrun that bear,' he said.

"The man looked up from his shoes. 'I don't have to outrun the bear,' he said, 'I only have to outrun you.'"

It seemed funny at the time, but that was before we faced a bear ourselves.

Dodger and I had been friends for a long time. Our families were friends. Even though we were different, we liked each other. Dodger was athletic; he was on every team there was. I was better in school; I had even won the speech contest at school by memorizing and delivering the entire Gettysburg address.

One thing we both liked to do was to camp, and every summer our families went on a camping trip together to Little Bear Mountain.

As we hiked along the trail that day, Dodger told jokes, and I listened and laughed. It had been a quiet day. Our parents had cooked breakfast, and before we left they had given us instructions for bear safety.

"Make a lot of noise," they said. "If you see any evidence of a bear, turn and come right back."

I wasn't worried. As many times as we had hiked this trail, we had never seen a bear. And anyway we knew what to do:

Stay calm.
Back away slowly.
Talk calmly and firmly.
Leave the area, if possible.

We came around a bend to a clearing, still laughing from the latest joke, and there she was—a large black bear with two small cubs.

She stood on her hind legs and sniffed the air. Dodger froze beside me. I froze, too. I tried to remember our survival skills. "Stay calm" had seemed easy on paper but now seemed almost impossible. My heart was racing in my chest.

The bear dropped on all fours and charged toward us. She skidded to a halt about ten yards away.

Dodger grabbed my arm. My knees were weak with fear. The bear stopped and swung her head to the side, then back and forth. Her eyes were glowing in anger. Her teeth were enormous.

I remembered the next tip: "Don't run." That was easy. Our feet were planted to the ground in terror.

The third was harder: "Talk."

What do you say to a 200-pound bear? My mind was blank with fear, and my mouth was dry as dust. Suddenly Abraham Lincoln's words popped into my mind.

"Fourscore and seven years ago," I said weakly. The bear stared at me intensely. I made my voice louder, "Our fathers brought forth upon this continent a new nation . . ."

"Keep talking," Dodger whispered as he nudged me with his elbow.

"Conceived in liberty and dedicated to the proposition that all men are created equal!" My voice went up higher and higher, till I felt that I was screeching.

"Woof!" The bear made a barking noise at us as she backed up and slapped the ground. She stood up and swung her head from side to side again.

"More!" Dodger said.

"We are now engaged in a great civil war . . ."

She listened a few more seconds, then walked slowly out of the clearing with her cubs. The bears disappeared into the woods. I stopped my speech.

Everything seemed like a dream. The woods were so quiet. Dodger and I backed slowly out of the clearing and then took off. We didn't stop running until we were all the way back at the campsite, safe with our parents.

My dad went to the ranger station to report the incident, and we moved our campsite to the other side of the mountain. Still, Dodger and I didn't do any more hiking that trip.

When I remember that bear—her eyes, those teeth—and the fear, I'm just glad to be alive! That is my SOS. Thank you, Abraham Lincoln!

Mrs. Meany

by Robbie Robinson

The old lady across the road is named Meany. Mrs. Meany. And she sure lives up to her name. She's the meanest woman in the county, in the state, in the world. Everybody says so.

Now, I've got a goat named Billy. Here's how I got him. My friend Tom's family was moving to the city, and you can't have goats inside the city limits, so he asked me if I wanted Billy. I said, "I'll ask my mom."

My mom's a writer. I always wait till she's writing to ask for things, because she says, "Yes, but don't bother me."

So I went in and said, "Mom, can I have a goat?" She said, "Yes, but don't bother me," and when she came downstairs an hour later, there was Billy.

"Where did that come from?" she asked.

"Mom, it's my goat. You said I could keep him."

"I did not."

"You did! I said, 'Mom, can I have a goat?' and you said, 'Yes, but don't bother me.'"

"I'll tell you one thing," Mom said. "You better keep him out of Mrs. Meany's yard. You don't want to get on the wrong side of Mrs. Meany."

I said, "I didn't know Mrs. Meany had a right side. I'll keep him fenced up in the back yard," and that's what I did.

Only, one hot summer day the gate was left open, and the next time I looked out the front window, Billy was disappearing into Mrs. Meany's cornfield.

I ran across the road. Then I pretended to be just strolling along, calling quietly, "Billy, come on, Billy. Do you want to get killed, Billy?"

I could hear rustling deep in the field, and I knew I had to go in after him. I slipped inside one of the rows.

It was August, and the corn was way over my

head. It was like being in a forest, and I kept going deeper and deeper. I'd hear a noise over there, and I'd go that way. A noise over here, and I'd go here. Pretty soon I stopped. I didn't hear anything.

This was a big cornfield. I was in the middle of it, and not only couldn't I find my goat, I was lost. It was like being in a maze. This is how rats must feel.

At last I heard a noise.

"Billy, Billy! Over here!"

The noise got closer.

"Over here, Billy! But keep quiet or the old hag will—"

At that moment the corn parted, and there stood the old hag. We looked at each other, and all of a sudden the corn just started spinning around me. I felt like I was in a whirlpool, twirling down a drain of green water.

I knew what was happening. All the men on my dad's side of the family have been known to faint. When Mom gave birth to me, it was Dad who passed out. My uncle fainted in the army, right in front of the general. Granddad fainted watching eye surgery on TV.

I didn't stay out very long—not as long as I'd have liked. When I came to, I could hear Mrs. Meany's voice. She was talking to somebody.

"Well, do you think he needs mouth-to-mouth resuscitation?"

"Baaaa."

She was talking to the goat. About me! About mouth-to-mouth resuscitation.

I opened my eyes fast.

Mrs. Meany said—still talking to the goat—"Do you think he can get up by himself, or does he need a hand?"

Billy said, "Baaaa."

I struggled to my feet.

"Follow me," Mrs. Meany said to the goat.

And she led the way out of the cornfield. I followed. When we got out to the road, she said to Billy, "Now you keep him out of my corn, you hear?"

Billy said, "Baaaa."

I said, "Thank you," and Billy and I went home.

I never will forget that day—my SOS day—because of three things:

1. I stopped being afraid of Mrs. Meany,
2. I learned that goats know what's being said to them, and
3. I passed out like a man.

Wanted: SOS

by Corky Cadenhead

Mr. Magro, I have watched all week as everyone else has gone to the front of the room and slipped a story into the SOS folder.

I just watched, because when you gave us the assignment, more than anything else in the world I wanted to write an SOS—but my mind went blank. It seems that nothing ever happens to me.

That night I took my notebook along with me while I baby-sat the twins, and just as I was getting out my pencil the twins yelled. They had locked themselves in the bathroom. I had to call the fire department to get them out. A fireman had to go through the window on a giant ladder. How could I ever come up with an SOS with all that going on?

When I got home, I tried again. I got in my favorite thinking chair and closed my eyes to concentrate. Then . . . "Rrowww!" A terrible noise came from the laundry room. My cat, Pumpkin, had crawled into the dryer between loads and got fluffed up. When I took her out, she looked like a giant dandelion. My concentration was broken. No SOS.

I tried to think about it at school, but everything that happened was too distracting. I burped in the spelling bee and got disqualified. Then I went to return Miss Jenkin's thesaurus and discovered that my dog, Arlo, had chewed the corner off. Then at lunch Willie Howell's milk tipped over into my lap, and my mother had to come to school to bring me clean pants. How could I write with all that going on?

That weekend my dad and I went camping with the Indian Princesses. I took my notebook with me hoping for inspiration to strike. That night we all told ghost stories and then were too afraid to go to the bathroom in the dark (even my dad). Later a mouse got into our snack food and hopped over our sleeping bags in the dark. You should have heard Dad scream.

This morning my paper was still blank. I thought all the way to school, but right before we turned into the parking lot my mom rear-ended a plumbing truck and all the pipes rolled onto our car. So here I am, writing down all my excuses instead of an SOS.

I just wanted you to know, Mr. Magro, that my SOS is this assignment—I have no SOS! As soon as I have an emergency, I'll be writing to you about it.

Miracle on Main Street

by Joy Frazure

I had about as bad a start in life as a girl can have. I was born in the Main Street Motel—at least that's what they say—and almost immediately I was wrapped up in a motel towel and thrown in the Dumpster behind the office.

That could have been the end of me. I could have been hauled away to the dump. And even if that didn't happen, it was the morning of November 2, and a cold front was supposed to come through at noon.

Well, people started packing up their cars to leave the motel next morning, and there was this one man, a salesman, who had parked near the Dumpster, and he heard a faint sound and stopped.

"Somebody's put a kitten in that Dumpster," he said, shaking his head. He got in his truck and started the engine, and then he turned it off and got out. "I'm a fool, but I'm going to get that kitten out of there."

He stood on the fender, reached into the Dumpster, and pulled me out. "Look at that, look at that!" He couldn't believe that somebody would put a baby in a Dumpster.

Everything happened fast after that. The motel people sent for an ambulance and the police, and I was taken to the hospital.

They had a big write-up in the local paper, but nobody claimed me or came forward. The police tried to trace everybody who had been at the motel that night, but not everybody had given their right names. So all the information I had about that night was the write-up that was in the newspaper. It's pasted on the first page of my scrapbook.

I was in the hospital for a week, they tell me, and then I was adopted by the best family in the world. It was my mom and dad who told me all about that night and about the man.

"I wish I could find that man" was what I said every time I looked at my scrapbook. A picture of him standing by the Dumpster was in the newspaper, but they didn't print his name.

You can imagine how often I thought about that man. If it hadn't been for him, I wouldn't be here. I wouldn't be alive.

So one day I was looking at the picture, and I saw that the man had on a jumpsuit with something printed on the pocket. I couldn't make out what it was, so I said to my mom, "I think that man's name is embroidered on his pocket." My mom got a magnifying glass, but we couldn't make it out.

I said, "I'm going to the newspaper. They'll have the original."

My mom said, "Maybe not, hon. It's been a long time."

I said, "I got to try."

My mom drove me thirty miles to the next town, where the newspaper was printed. As we walked in, I said, "I want to do the talking."

My mom said, "If that's what you really want, hon."

I did hold her hand for support as I went up to the receptionist and explained what I wanted. I got to see the editor right away.

He said, "We might still have the original." He made some phone calls, and finally a man came up and laid an old manila envelope on the editor's desk. He pulled out two photographs. The first one was just a shot of the motel, but the second was the one I had in my scrapbook. You could read the writing on the suit without a magnifying glass—WONDER CAKES AND PIES.

I was disappointed because I had wanted a name, but the editor punched some buttons and said, "Martha, pull up Wonder Cakes and Pies on your computer and see if they're still in business." He waited, listened, and said, "The home office is in Atlanta. I'll put one of my reporters on it for you. It would be a good human-interest story."

"No, sir," I said. "This is private, but I thank you for your help."

He gave me the address of Wonder Cakes and Pies and the eight-by-ten picture of the man at the motel.

The next week, my mom and dad drove me to Atlanta. They went with me into Wonder Cakes and Pies, but they let me do the talking. As soon as I explained my situation, I got to see the president of the company. I couldn't have been prouder if he was the president of the United States.

He took one look at the picture and said, "Get Robinson in here. Robinson's head of the sales department."

Robinson came in quick. The president handed him the picture. "Give me a name."

"Fred Mullins."

At hearing the name I had wanted to know for so long, my eyes filled with tears and I had to sit down.

"Fred retired last year," Mr. Robinson went on, "but I believe he's still in Atlanta. I can get his address for you if it's important."

"It's the most important thing in the world," I said.

We got the address and directions, and Mom and Dad and I drove over there. Someone from the office must have called Mr. Mullins to tell him we were coming, because he was waiting out on the porch.

I jumped out of the car and ran across the yard. "Do you know who I am?"

He said, "I haven't seen you since you were one day old, but I'd know you anywhere." And he held out his arms, and I went right inside.

When I could finally talk, I said, "All my life I've wanted to know you and tell you just one thing."

He said, "What's that?"

I said, "I thank you with all my heart."

After that, we went into the house and had a celebration. Fred Mullins told his part of the story. Mom and Dad told theirs, and I told mine.

It was one of the happiest days of my life. He said it was one of the happiest days of his, too.

Mom and Dad and I got back in the car, and Mom said, "What a nice man."

I said, "I've known that all my life."

And we drove home.

Shark
Food

by Red Fletcher

SHARK DIVE the sign said in big letters.

"Hey, let's sign up for a shark dive," I said to my dad.

"Shark dive? Are you sure you want to?"

Dad is a scuba-diving instructor. *Scuba* means self-contained underwater breathing apparatus. He's always up for adventure, but I could tell he was worried about me.

I had seen *Jaws* on TV several times. And recently I had read an article entitled "Man-Eater Shark: The Terror of the Sea," but I didn't think about that then.

"Of course I'm sure," I said. "The sign says they take groups out every day. It's perfectly safe or they wouldn't do it. Right?"

Dad was convinced.

On the day of the dive we loaded our gear onto the boat and headed out. There were ten of us in the group. Our dive master, Shadrach, briefed us as we rode to the site.

"Sharks are dangerous animals. We must respect them," he said.

He didn't need to tell me that. I did respect sharks. They are the most powerful animals in the sea, and they have several sets of very sharp teeth. They can kill their prey in a single bite, but I tried not to think about that. We would be diving with reef sharks, which aren't as dangerous as some other shark species.

"Weight yourself down with at least two to four pounds of extra weight," Shadrach instructed. "That way you will sink straight to the bottom and not float up. When you reach the bottom, form a circle. I will stand in the middle and feed the sharks. Hold still. No flailing around while I am feeding the sharks."

"What's flailing?" I whispered to Dad.

Dad flapped his arms at his side. "Swinging your arms around like this."

Shadrach continued, "If your arms are swinging around, then the shark might think you've got food, and your arm might end up being shark food." He laughed.

I didn't think it was so funny. I looked down at my arm and wiggled my fingers. I made a mental note to be perfectly still under the water and keep my arms close to my sides at all times.

Shadrach leaned toward me. "Hey, the sharks, they like the red hair." He laughed, then yelled to the group, "Okay, get ready."

I hooked up my gear and checked my air supply. Three thousand pounds of air. Plenty!

I put on my weight belt. I figured the seven pounds that I already had would be enough, so I didn't add any extra weight.

We lined up on the end of the boat. I smoothed back my hair. My dad punched me in the arm and pointed over the side. I leaned over and looked. Sharks were swimming all around the boat. They looked the way they do in the movies. Restless.

"Ready?" Shadrach called.

"Ready," we answered.

Shadrach pulled down his mask and jumped in. We followed.

Immediately, we began sinking to the bottom, with sharks swimming all around us. They were much bigger than I had expected. And their eyes looked like white beads with thin black slits in the middle.

Some of the sharks had small suckerfish attached to their sides. One shark had a fishing hook hanging out of its mouth.

We settled into our positions in the circle on the bottom. The sharks swam in and out between the divers. Shadrach placed his thumb and first finger together forming a circle and held it up, giving us the "okay" sign. We did the same to say we were fine. Then Shadrach pulled a piece of fish from the feeding box and held it out. A large shark swung around and snatched the fish. The other sharks immediately began to swim faster, more frantic. Several sharks swam right by me, very close.

Shadrach pulled out another fish, which was grabbed by a small shark. Some of the sharks bumped Shadrach with their noses. The sharks were circling fast now, around the divers.

Sharks were swimming very close to me, but I wasn't frightened, just a bit tense. Then, unfortunately, I began to float up slightly. Automatically, I swung my arm up trying to force myself back down. As I did, a small shark passed by. It was the shark with the hook in his mouth. He gave my

arm a sideways glance. Shadrach's words rang in my ears: "Your arm might end up being shark food."

I needed to yell SOS, but you can't talk underwater, so I had to do something myself.

How could I make myself stay on the bottom? More weight. I quickly scanned the bottom for a rock that I could slip into the pocket of my vest to weight me down. No rocks anywhere.

"Breathe slowly and steadily," I told myself. "Stay relaxed."

The only other solution I could think of was to release any extra air that might be in my buoyancy vest. I held up the air tube on my vest and pushed the release button. Bubbles escaped from the end of the tube, and I felt myself sink lower. My knees settled on the sandy bottom. I quickly tucked my arms by my sides and left them there. Not available for shark food!

Shadrach held out another piece of fish. The largest shark snatched it and swam by. He didn't give me a second glance, which is just the way I like it.

Identity Crisis

by Gipper Saunders

Some things are better when they are new. Video games fresh out of the cellophane, spiral notebooks on the first day of school, or brand-new tennis shoes.

Other things are better old: soft worn-out jeans, leather baseball gloves, and especially baseball caps.

Mine was perfect. That cap was a part of me as much as my blue eyes or crooked smile. It was part of who I was. Years of molding and wear had worn it down just to the perfect shape of my head. Sun, rain, and sweat had ripened it from its original dark navy to a soft gray. And it had history. We had been through a lot together. Ball games and summer days. I kept it on a peg by the back door and never went anywhere without it.

"Yucky!" Sammy, the four-year-old next door, would say, pointing to my cap on the peg. He followed me everywhere I went. He even tried to dress like me.

"Yep, yucky," I would answer, smiling at Sammy. The brim was worn, the cardboard peeking through. Duct tape held the back together. In other words, it was perfect.

Then one day my SOS happened.

I went outside and reached for my cap. The peg was empty.

"Mom!" I yelled. "My cap, where is it?"

My mother came out onto the porch and shook her head. "I don't know," she said. Then she frowned. "I hope . . .," she began.

"Hope what, Mom?"

"Well, maybe . . .," she stopped.

I pleaded. "Tell me!"

"I left some things out here for the church thrift shop, and I guess they took the cap, too, by mistake."

SOS!

My mom drove me all the way down to the

thrift shop, and we went through every box and bag. We found the box of my family's old things, but the cap wasn't there. I almost cried.

"We sold it," they told us when we asked. "Actually, we gave it away. A boy and his mother came by and chose it right off the bat."

The woman working at the thrift shop felt so sorry for me that she found me another cap.

"Here," the woman said. "We have this one that came in last week, and it's brand-new." She held up a Braves cap and smiled.

"Thanks," I said weakly. I bent the brim and rolled it around, then put the cap on my head. It sat up high and stiff—as uncomfortable as a new pair of Sunday shoes.

I walked out of the thrift shop a different person. My identity was at stake. That Braves cap was like a beacon of newness on my head. I was in misery.

I was sitting in my kitchen, not wanting to go outside anymore, when I saw it—my cap bobbed by the window. I rubbed my eyes and looked again. The cap bobbed up again. Someone was running through my back yard in my cap. I ran outside.

"Sammy!" I yelled out the back door.

"Yeah?"

"Where did you get that cap?"

"Yucky!" Sammy said, patting the cap on his head and smiling.

I needed the cap back, but I didn't want to hurt Sammy's feelings.

"Sammy." I sat down beside him. "The important thing about a cap is that you have to make it old *yourself*, see?" I took off my new cap and held it out. "When my cap started, it looked just like this."

"It did?"

"It did."

"And it got worn out, aged to perfection on my head. Want your own yucky cap?"

Sammy nodded.

I put my old cap on my head. It settled down like a familiar friend. I put the new Braves cap on Sammy's head. It slipped down over his eyes.

"Yucky," I said.

"Yucky," he answered proudly.

Together we went to get the duct tape.

White Lightning

by Ima Writer

(Mr. Magro, this is really me, Brianna Thompson, but I decided to have a pen name. I hope that's all right.)

This was the summer I had been waiting for. This summer White Lightning would be all mine.

When Granny and Granddad got the horse they said, "Now, the horse belongs to all three of you, share and share alike."

We shared him for five summers, but this year my sister Ellie was married. My brother Johnny was at college on a football scholarship. Lightning was all mine!

That first afternoon, as soon as I unpacked my clothes, I went out and got Lightning out of the barn. We headed down to the river. Now, Lightning didn't exactly live up to his name. It was like he was happiest just walking along, enjoying the trees and the breeze. If it were left up to him, he'd never trot or canter or gallop.

My granny yelled, "Brianna?"

I stopped and looked back.

"No swimming," she called after me.

"Granny, I haven't even got on my bathing suit."

Granny was always worried about the river. One of her cousins had drowned on a family picnic, and we were not allowed to swim unless an adult was watching us.

Anyway, I was not going swimming.

Lightning and I stopped at the river by the tire swing. My granddad had made this tire swing when we were little. He and Granny even took turns on it—to see if it was strong enough, they claimed.

I slid off Lightning's back—I hadn't bothered with a saddle—and got on the tire swing. I went far out over the water. I felt so good. The wind was in my face. My horse was grazing at the edge of the water.

I swung out over the water two times, three.

On the fourth time, when I was as far out over the river as the swing would go, there was a sound like a rifle shot right in my ear. I plunged into the water.

I had used up all my breath screaming as I fell, and I couldn't get to the surface to breathe because I was still half in the tire. Just as I finally came up, the limb crashed down. It hit me hard on the shoulder, and I went under.

I went way under the water this time. I struggled up, but there was something wrong with my shoulder, and my left arm wouldn't work.

I got my head above the water and gulped in some air, but I went right under again. This time I didn't think I would ever come up again. I kicked hard with my feet, and my face broke the surface of the water. I gulped air and tried to kick toward the shore.

I was in the middle of the river by now, though, and land looked far away. I could see Lightning on the shore. He wasn't grazing anymore. He was looking in my direction. I tried to choke out the word "Lightning," but I went under before I could. Even though I hadn't been able to get the word out, maybe he heard my silent SOS.

(I know you think this is too many "went

under"s, Mr. Magro, but that's how many there really were. Don't worry, there are only two more.)

As I bobbed up I heard a splash, and I knew Lightning was coming toward me. He was a good swimmer, but—just like on land—he was taking his time about it, and I didn't think he would reach me in time.

I went under and came up again. This time my good arm brushed Lightning's face. I grabbed for his mane and missed. I went under again. This time when I came up, Lightning was there, right beside me. I grabbed his mane with my good arm, and we headed for the shore.

I let go in the shallow water and struggled up the bank by myself. I got to my feet. My left arm was dangling at my side like it might never work again. I couldn't get on Lightning's back with just one good arm, so I held on to him for support, and we started slowly for home.

Gran came running out of the kitchen when she saw me. "I told you not to go—" I started crying, and she didn't finish what she'd been about to say. She helped me into the house.

(All this really happened, Mr. Magro, and the only thing I changed was the horse's name. His name wasn't really White Lightning. His name was Bob.)

Pumpkin Man

by Kyle Weathers

It all started at camp last summer, when Joe and Wes and I decided to climb up the hill behind our cabin. We were almost to the top, when my hand grabbed some loose dirt. Suddenly, yellow-jackets were everywhere. Joe screamed. We ran.

This was my *first* SOS!

We ran to the swimming pool and jumped in. The water felt good on my forehead, which was burning. I felt several bumps over my left eye.

I stayed under water as long as I could.

When I came up the yellow-jackets were gone. Joe and Wes were rubbing themselves all over, as if that would rub off the stings. My left eye felt funny. I touched it. It felt huge.

Then Wes said, "Hey, look at Kyle."

Joe said, "Whoooooooaaaaaaaaa. Kyle, your eye is huge. You better go to the infirmary."

I couldn't see at all out of my left eye, and only a little out of my right.

That was my *second* SOS!!

We went to the infirmary, and the nurse gave me a tablet of Benadryl and an ice pack to put on my eye. I stayed in the infirmary. Wes stayed with me. The nurse gave me a mirror. My eyes were swollen shut, and my face was red.

"I look like something out of a horror movie," I said.

"Hey, you look like Pumpkin Man," Wes said.

Pumpkin Man was the legend around the camp. It was a campfire story about a headless man who roamed the hills with a pumpkin where his head should be.

We laughed, and I held my arms over my head and did a Pumpkin Man imitation. We both agreed I was the perfect Pumpkin Man.

Finally, the nurse said I was out of danger and we could go back to the cabin.

I still couldn't see much because of the swelling, and it was dark outside, so Wes led the

way. Halfway back to the cabin I realized I had for-
gotten my jacket.

"I'll go back and get it," Wes said. He placed my
hand on the side of a building. "This is the restroom. You wait here."

In the distance I could hear the campers singing
around the evening campfire. Standing there,
leaning against the building, I realized I had to go
to the restroom.

I felt my way around the building and inside. I
felt the sinks, then the stalls. I pushed a stall door
open and made my way in. Outside I heard the
noise of campers talking and laughing. Campfire
was over, and everyone was heading back to the
cabins.

I figured any minute the restroom would fill up
with guys, and we'd all have a laugh about the
yellow-jackets and my distorted Pumpkin Man
face. I unzipped my pants and was ready to go.

I heard the restroom door open and a crowd
enter, but it didn't sound like guys. There was lots
of laughing and giggling. It sounded like girls!

Suddenly a terrible truth struck me—I was in
the girls' restroom!

SOS number three!!!

I panicked. I couldn't remember if I had locked
my stall. I quickly turned and felt along the door
to hook the lock. I found it just in time. There

was a shove on the door, and a girl said, "Anyone in there?"

"Yes," I said in a high squeaky voice.

Suddenly it seemed like the place was packed with a million girls.

"Hey, hurry up," a girl yelled, pushing on my door.

"What's taking so long?" another yelled.

It wouldn't be long before they found me out. I had to get out of there, and I didn't have many options. If I had had my sight, I would have opened the door and run. I couldn't do that.

I had an idea. I had two things going for me— the element of surprise and my gross face. I knew what to do.

I pulled off my T-shirt so no one would recognize me. I tucked it in my jeans pocket. I gently unlocked my stall door and counted to three. With as much force as I could muster, I threw open my door and leaped out into the room. I held my arms over my head and growled as loud and as scary as I could.

"P u m p k i i i i i i i i i i i n n n n n n n Maaaaaaaaaaaaaaan!"

The screams were deafening. Girls were stampeding to get out.

"P u m p k i i i i i i i i i i i n n n n n n n Maaaaaaaaaaaaaaan!"

Girls cleared out like you wouldn't believe.

I quickly felt my way to the door and pushed it open.

"Wes," I yelled.

Wes grabbed my arm. "Let's get out of here," he said.

We hurried back to our cabin and fell on the bed laughing.

Mr. Magro, do I get triple extra credit for having three SOSs? ☺

Held
Back

by Anonymous

*"Class, each of you has now read your SOS.
Here is the final one. It's called 'Held Back.'"*
"Held back, like in school, Mr. Magro?"
"Yes."
"Someone in this room?"
"Yes. Stop looking around and listen."

I don't know a worse SOS than being held back
in first grade. And I was.

Being held back was humiliating because I was
big. Worst of all, my little sister was across the
hall in first grade. She was already ahead of me in
reading. Everybody was.

Well, the first week our teacher, Mrs. Kincaid, had us draw pictures of our families and sign our names. She handed back the papers, calling out the names: "Sara . . . Bobby . . . Freddie . . . Mot." She stopped and read it again. "Mot." No one came up to get the paper. "Do we have a Mot?"

Everyone laughed. Finally all the papers were handed out, and I didn't have one. Mrs. Kincaid gave me a smile and came back and put the paper on my desk.

When the bell rang, Mrs. K stopped me and asked me to stay for a minute. I stayed. She complimented me on my picture but didn't say a word about my name.

She had figured out right away what was wrong—I was dyslexic. Words looked backward to me. We worked together. She started out by letting me draw. I was good at that. Then she had me label the pictures. Pretty soon I was doing cartoons with dialogue.

Because of Mrs. Kincaid, not only did I pass first grade but I was able to finish high school and college. I even became a teacher. Now, when I sign my cartoons I always sign them MOT.

"It's you, Mr. Magro! You were held back in first grade."

"Yes."

"I didn't know you were held back."

"I was."

"I didn't know you could be a teacher if you were held back."

"You can be anything you want if you work hard."

"And I guess you don't get extra credit because you're the teacher."

"Right. I give all the credit to Mrs. Kincaid, who answered my SOS."

CPSIA information can be obtained at www.ICGtesting.com
Printed in the USA
LVOW11s1552030314

375861LV00002B/421/P